Full Moon Fever

Look for more books in the Goosebumps Series 2000 by R.L. Stine:

And coming soon:

Full Moon Fever

R.L. Stine

SCHOLASTIC

Scholastic Children's Books
Commonwealth House, 1–19 New Oxford Street, London WC1A 1NU, UK
a division of Scholastic Ltd
London ~ New York ~ Toronto ~ Sydney ~ Auckland
Mexico City ~ New Delhi ~ Hong Kong

First published in the USA by Scholastic Inc., 1999
First published in the UK by Scholastic Ltd, 2000

ISBN 0 439 01348 8

Typeset by Rowland Phototypesetting Ltd, Bury St Edmunds, Suffolk
Printed by Mackays of Chatham plc, Chatham, Kent

10 9 8 7 6 5 4 3 2 1

My sister, Alesha, tilted back her head, closed her bright blue eyes, and opened her mouth in a long, high, animal howl.

I took a deep breath and began to howl with her. I cupped my hands round my open mouth and howled louder, my shrill wail mixing with Alesha's.

"*Owoooooooooooo!*"

Scruffy, our long-haired dachshund, tilted his brown head at the sound. Then he reared on to his stubby back legs — and began to bark ferociously.

The longer we howled, the more he barked.

Mum's angry cry rose over our wails. "Robbie — Alesha — stop torturing the dog!"

Alesha and I cut off our howls. We collapsed laughing on to the living room carpet. Scruffy let out a few more yips. The little guy was panting hard, his tail whipping to and fro furiously.

1

I grabbed him off the floor with both hands, fell on to my back, and pulled him on top of me. He began licking my face. I think he was begging me not to howl any more.

"You know that Scruffy hates it when you howl like that. Why do you enjoy torturing the dog so much?" Mum demanded, frowning at us from the doorway.

"Because it's fun," I replied.

For some reason, that struck both Alesha and me as funny, and we started laughing all over again.

"You two are about as funny as chapped lips," Mum said. It was one of her expressions. She said it all the time. "Why don't you pick on someone your own size?"

"Okay," I replied. "I'll pick on Alesha." I grabbed my sister by the shoulders and wrestled her to the floor.

She let out a cry and punched me in the gut.

Scruffy jumped on her and began barking again, trying to protect me.

"Get up!" Mum cried. "Get over here. Check your overnight bags. See if I've packed everything you want."

Alesha and I both groaned.

We're both tall and a little bit chubby. Actually, we're about the same height even though I'm twelve and she's eleven. We both have straight black hair and round blue eyes.

And we're both really good groaners and complainers. And proud of it!

"Why do we have to go and see Grandpa John tonight?" I whined.

Dad appeared behind Mum, lugging the two canvas overnight bags. He answered my question. "Because he's lonely. Because he doesn't have kids around the house any more. Because he looks forward to seeing you two."

"But he's always telling us the most frightening stories!" Alesha exclaimed.

"Grandpa John always tries to scare us," I said.

Dad dropped the bags by the front door and frowned at us. "But you told me you *like* being scared — remember?"

"Well . . . yeah," I replied. I climbed off the floor and crossed the room to check my bag.

Dad was right. Alesha and I like scary movies and books. And we like making up frightening stories to terrify the two kids we babysit for over the street.

It's just turned October, and we've already started planning some really gross Halloween costumes.

We *do* like scary things. But Grandpa John is a little *too* scary.

I mean, he looks so weird. He's really tall, bony, and pale. He always reminds me of some kind of big insect — a pale white spider or a

3

praying mantis, hunched over, with his skinny, stick arms, scraping his hands together, staring at us with bulging, watery eyes.

Grandpa John lives by himself in a little cottage deep in the woods. Alesha and I can never get to sleep when we stay there. The wind always howls, and we hear animals creeping about and strange cries and moans right outside our bedroom windows.

But that's not the only reason we can't get to sleep. Every time we visit, Grandpa John waits until really late at night. And then he builds a big, crackling fire in his old stone fireplace. And he tells us the most terrifying stories — stories that give us nightmares for weeks.

Stories he claims are true.

Like the story of the headless fifth grader who kept coming to school every day — even though the other kids had chopped his head off and buried it in the playground.

Or the story of the Bottom Feeders — two girls who drowned but lived on as zombies. They survived underwater by eating stuff off the lake bottom. And for fun, they grabbed swimmers by the ankles and pulled them down to the bottom to live with them for ever.

Nice stories, huh?

"These pyjamas don't fit me any more," Alesha complained, pulling them out of her bag and tossing them across the room. "Why

4

did you pack them? You know I can't wear them."

"Well, go upstairs and pick out your own pyjamas." Mum sighed.

"Why can't Scruffy come too?" I demanded, petting the little guy, scratching him behind the ears. "Scruffy would like being in the woods."

"Oh, yeah. For sure." Dad rolled his eyes. "Scruffy is a real outdoors type of dog. He's afraid of *leaves*!" He and Mum burst out laughing.

"Ha ha," I muttered. "He's not afraid of all leaves — only *big* leaves."

I picked Scruffy up. "Come on, boy. We're going to Grandpa John's."

"Put him down," Mum scolded. "You know why Scruffy can't come. Grandpa John is allergic to dogs. They make him sneeze and break out in a rash."

"Ah — ah —" I opened my mouth, shut my eyes, and faked a really loud sneeze. "AHHHH-CHHHOOOO!"

Alesha laughed as she stuffed a nightshirt into her duffle bag.

"I'm allergic to Grandpa John!" I declared. "Maybe I'd better stay at home with Scruffy."

"Nice try," Dad said sarcastically. "Let's pack up the car. It's getting late."

I let out a sigh and lowered Scruffy to the

floor. Then I grabbed my jacket, picked up my bag and started outside.

I stepped out into a clear, cold night. I could see my breath steam in front of me. It felt more like winter than the beginning of October.

And as I made my way to the car in the driveway, a cold shiver swept down my back.

Why did I have such a bad feeling about this visit to Grandpa John?

Why did I think this might be our scariest visit yet?

The drive to Grandpa John's house took about an hour. Alesha and I spent the time in the back seat arguing about our Halloween costumes.

"You can't *both* be giant, furry bugs from outer space!" Mum declared.

"Where are you going to get the fur?" Dad chimed in.

"We'll shave Scruffy!" I joked.

"That's about as funny as chapped lips," Mum said.

Dad turned off the road and followed the dirt driveway that led to Grandpa John's cottage in the woods. Grandpa John was waiting in the doorway. Behind him, I could see the orange glow of a fire in the fireplace.

Grandpa John was wearing khaki overalls and a red flannel shirt. He came loping out with that stiff-legged grasshopper walk of his. His head bobbed up and down with each stride. His long, straight white hair fluttered in the wind.

He pulled open the back door of the car and leaned inside, peering in at Alesha and me with his bulging bug eyes. "Well, well, well," he said, grinning.

"How are you, Grandpa John?" I asked, sliding out of the car. I shivered in the icy air.

Grandpa John scraped his hands together. "Welcome to my home, *said the spider to the fly*!" His grin grew wider.

The wind made the trees shake and whisper. A pale half-moon floated low in a cloudy sky. In the light of the car headlights, I saw a big field mouse scamper round the side of the cottage.

I shivered again.

Late at night, whenever I sleep at Grandpa John's, I always hear the scrape of tiny feet over the wooden rafters above my head. The cottage must be filled with those big brown mice, I realized.

After hugs and greetings all round, Grandpa John led us into the cottage. It was warm inside. A pine cone popped loudly in the fireplace, sending yellow sparks flying. The house smelled of stale tobacco smoke. Grandpa John smoked his pipe every night after dinner.

"Is that a new armchair?" Dad asked, pointing to a wide, lumpy, green leather chair in front of the fireplace.

Grandpa John nodded. "Some animal got in

the house. Raccoon, I think. Scratched my old chair to bits."

Alesha gulped. "Did you chase the raccoon out?"

Grandpa John scratched the top of his white hair. "I think it left. I haven't seen it."

He turned to me. "I've got those snack cakes you like, Robbie. And I'm going to make us a big bowl of popcorn." He scraped his bony hands together. "Pig-out time!"

"Time for us to get going," Mum said. "Our dinner reservation is for eight. We're already late."

Mum and Dad always drop off Alesha and me, then hurry to their favourite restaurant in the next town. It gives Grandpa John lots of time to spend alone with us.

Time to scare us to death!

He walked them out to the car to say good-bye. A burst of cold air followed him in when he returned. He closed the door behind him and locked it.

"Cold night," he muttered, rubbing the sleeves of his flannel shirt. "Let me pop the popcorn. Then we'll warm up in front of the fire."

A few minutes later, he had spread a plate of snack cakes, a big bowl of popcorn, and two tall glasses of apple juice on the low table in front of us.

Alesha and I sat on the edge of the worn

leather sofa, leaning forward to reach the food. The flames danced and jumped in the fireplace. I could feel the heat on my face and through my sweater.

Grandpa John settled into his new armchair. The chair made a *WHOOSH* sound as he sat down. He grinned at us, watching us gobble handfuls of popcorn. The fire cast darting shadows over him.

He picked up his pipe, smoothed his hand over it a few times, then set it back down. "It's almost Halloween," he said softly. "Are you two ready for a story? I have a good story for Halloween."

I started to reply. But a shrill animal howl interrupted.

It sounded so close — right outside the front window of the cottage.

"What was that?" I cried.

I listened for another howl. But heard only silence now.

Grandpa John leaned forward in the big chair. "Maybe it's the wind in the trees," he replied, his voice just above a whisper. "Or maybe . . . maybe it's someone who caught Full Moon Fever."

I gasped. "Full Moon Fever? What's that?"

3

A twig snapped in the fire. A burning log broke and fell, sending up a shower of red-and-yellow sparks.

The shadows danced over Grandpa John's face. The firelight reflected in his large, wet eyes.

"It's a long story," he replied finally. He cleared his throat. His big hands spread like spiders over the arms of the chair.

I took a big handful of popcorn and settled back on the sofa.

Sitting beside me, Alesha had her hands tightly clasped in her lap. Her eyes were locked on Grandpa John.

"The story takes place a year ago," he began. "Last October. You might remember that I was travelling then. I spent some time in Canada. Deep in the north woods. Hiking and camping."

"Was it cold?" Alesha interrupted. She leaned forward to pick up her glass of juice.

11

Grandpa John tapped his fingers on the arms of the chair. He didn't like to be interrupted when he told one of his stories. I think Alesha did it just to annoy him.

"It was cold but pleasant," he told her. "The air smelled like pine, so fresh and clean. The hills sparkled, green as emeralds."

He cleared his throat again. "I was having a wonderful time, wandering by myself through the pine forests. But one night, I walked away from my camp-site and lost the path in the darkness. The sun had gone down. The moon and stars were covered with clouds.

"Somehow I got totally lost. The tall pine trees surrounded me. I suddenly felt trapped, as if they were keeping me prisoner, hiding the path from me.

"I searched for an hour, maybe two. The batteries in my torch began to weaken. The light grew dim. I knew I was lost.

"I heard animal sounds in the trees. Low hoots and moans. I could hear the scrape of animal paws over the dead leaves, over the blanket of dried pine needles on the forest floor."

"Friendly animals? Or hungry animals?" Alesha asked.

"I don't know," Grandpa John replied. "I tried not to panic. But my heart was pounding in my chest. My fear had tightened my throat, made it so hard to swallow.

"It grew colder. The wind picked up. A howling wind, just like tonight. My teeth began to chatter.

"I *had* to find the path. My tent and all my supplies — they were at the top of the path.

"The hooting in the trees grew louder. I could hear the animal footsteps, following me as I walked.

"Finally, through the trunks of the tall pine trees, I saw a dim, flickering light up ahead. Firelight in the window of a tiny cabin.

"I cried out. I was so happy.

"I raced to the cabin and pounded on the wooden door. After a few seconds, an old woman pulled open the door. She gasped in fright when she saw me. My hair was wild about my face. I was panting hard. I must have been a sight!

"'I — I'm lost,' I managed to stammer through my chattering teeth.

"The old woman invited me inside. 'I don't get many visitors,' she said. She allowed me to stand in front of the fire until I warmed up. I leaned close to the fireplace. It took a long time for me to stop shaking.

"Then she sat me down at her wooden table and gave me a big, steaming bowl of soup. She was very kind. She explained that her husband was a hunter and trapper. They had lived deep

13

in the woods their entire lives. He was away, checking on his fur traps.

"We talked for a while. Then she gave me directions to find my way back to the path. I thanked her and stood up to leave. But she stopped me at the door.

"'Keep your eyes down as you walk,' she warned. 'It's a night for Full Moon Fever.'

"I turned back to her. I'd never heard of Full Moon Fever. I asked her to explain.

"She motioned for me to take my seat again at the table. I obeyed. The fire warmed my back as she sat opposite me, clasping her old, gnarled hands on the table. Dark shadows danced over her wrinkled face. But her grey eyes glowed brightly as she began to explain.

"'It's a full moon tonight,' she began. 'And when the full moon appears on Halloween night, it casts a special light. A dangerous light.'

"'How is it dangerous?' I asked.

"Her eyes burned into mine. 'If you gaze up at the full moon at just the right moment,' she warned, 'you will catch it. You will catch Full Moon Fever.'

"'It's an illness?' I demanded, leaning towards her over the table, feeling feverish already from the powerful heat of the fire.

"'It starts out as a fever,' the old woman explained, her voice growing shrill. 'Like a sudden case of the flu. But then your body starts to change.'

"A laugh escaped my throat. I guess it was a nervous laugh. 'You mean you become a *werewolf*?' I cried.

"She shook her head. 'When you catch Full Moon Fever, you become half-human, half-beast. You can no longer live with other humans. Because you are too hungry . . . too dangerously hungry.'

"I laughed again. Perhaps it was the intense expression on her old face, the glowing eyes, the clenched jaw. Such a crazy story, I thought. Just the kind of horror story an old woman in the middle of the forest would make up to frighten travellers.

"'Is there a cure?' I asked.

"She nodded. The glow faded from her eyes. 'Not an easy cure,' she whispered. 'You must wait twenty-eight days until the *next* full moon. And then you must raise your eyes to the moonlight at just the right moment.'

"'And that will cure Full Moon Fever?' I asked.

"She shut her eyes and sighed. 'I don't know. No one ever survives until the next full moon. . .'

"I stared at her for a long time, watching the shadows play over her face. Then I thanked her for the story and for her kindness.

"I stepped outside and took a few deep breaths of cold, fresh air. Beneath my parka, I could still feel the warmth of the fire on my back. And I could still see the old woman's glowing grey eyes in front of me as I began to make my way through the trees.

"I found myself chuckling as I followed her directions to the path. 'What a crazy story,' I murmured to myself. 'Why did she want to scare me? Probably just bored,' I decided.

"But her directions were good. I found the path easily. With a grateful sigh, I leaned into the wind and began to follow the path uphill.

"I had completely forgotten that it was indeed Halloween night.

"I gazed up at the sky. The clouds parted, revealing a bright full moon. It appeared to float so close . . . right over my head.

"As I gazed up at it, a flash of silver moonlight made me blink.

"The strange silver light washed over me. It felt so cold. Cold as ice.

"The silver light vanished. I suddenly felt dizzy.

"Rubbing my forehead with my gloved hand, I dropped to my knees.

"I felt sick. My stomach lurched.

"I began to sweat. My whole body shook. Chills made me shudder. But I felt so hot . . . so unbearably hot.

"And then my body started to change. My skin itched. Everything tingled and itched. My *eyeballs* itched!

"And then . . . I could feel the fur . . . pushing up, up through my skin. Thick, bristly fur, pushing up through my arms, my legs, my chest.

"I caught it, you see," Grandpa John said excitedly, leaning forward on the edge of the big armchair. "You understand what happened — don't you? Last Halloween in the woods, I caught Full Moon Fever!"

Alesha and I gaped at him in silence. His eyes were bulging. He was breathing rapidly.

With a furious growl, Grandpa John leaped off the chair — and dived at us.

"I caught Full Moon Fever!" he roared. "*And now I'm going to give it to YOU!*"

Alesha and I screamed.

I tried to escape, to dive off the sofa.

But Grandpa John's arms spread round us. Trapped us.

He threw back his head — and started to laugh. High, shrill laughter that sounded like a horse whinnying.

He held us both tight. When he finally stopped laughing, he had tears streaming down his face. A wide grin spread over his face.

"I *really* scared you that time!" he declared. "It was just a story. Just one of my stories!" And then he threw back his head and laughed some more.

I uttered an angry growl and pulled free of his grip.

Alesha scowled, shaking her head. "I — can't believe we fell for it," she whispered to me. Her hands were balled into tight fists. "I can't believe we let him scare us again."

"You kids are too easy," Grandpa John said, wiping the tears off his cheeks. "Too easy."

"I'm never going to fall for one of your stories again!" I told him.

His smile grew even wider. His eyes flashed. "We'll see," he said, chuckling.

We spent a restless night.

The light from the half-moon poured into my bedroom window, and I couldn't stop thinking about Full Moon Fever.

The next morning, I was glad when Mum came to pick us up.

Alesha and I pulled on our coats, said good-bye to Grandpa John, and hurried out of the front door.

Grandpa John followed us outside. "Hey, it's Halloween in two weeks," he called after us. "Remember, kids — don't look up at the full moon!"

Alesha and I shook our heads and groaned.

What a joker.

If only we had listened to him. . .

The week before Halloween, Alesha and I both caught the flu. We were in bed for days and didn't have the strength to work on our costumes.

So, on Halloween night we had to scurry around and put together some last-minute ideas.

Alesha dressed herself in a yellow sweatshirt and yellow tights. Then she taped a bright yellow plastic funnel upside down on her head. "I'm a Teletubby," she declared.

I folded a black sheet into a cape and found an old black mask and a plastic toy sword in my wardrobe. "Zorro," I announced.

"It's a little lame," Alesha said, frowning at me.

"At least I get to carry a sword," I replied.

"A baby sword with a rubber tip!" she sneered.

Why can't she ever give me a break?

I felt a strong tug at my cape. "Hey!" I cried out. "Scruffy — get off! Get off!"

The dog had its teeth clamped on the bottom of the cape and was growling and pulling, struggling to take it away from me.

"Did this dog go to Pest School?" I asked Alesha.

She laughed. "I think that's Scruffy's old sheet! He just wants it back."

Mum walked in as I gave Scruffy a little kick, trying to get him off the cape.

"Robbie — don't kick the dog!" she cried. "Why are you always torturing that poor dog?"

"I'm not!" I whined. "Scruffy is torturing *me*!"

Mum picked Scruffy up in both hands and raised him to her face. He licked her lips.

"Ohhh, yuck!" I groaned. "Dog kisses."

Mum let the dog kiss her a few more times. Wet, slurpy dog kisses. I think she did it just to make Alesha and me sick.

Finally, she turned back to me. "Who are you supposed to be? The Lone Ranger? You don't have a cowboy hat."

I uttered a low growl and tightened my hands into fists. "I'm Zorro," I muttered.

"Sorry." Mum lowered Scruffy to the floor. "And that sheet round your neck is a cape — right?"

"Right," I mumbled. "Doesn't it *look* like a cape?"

Mum didn't answer. Instead, she dropped to her knees beside Scruffy. "What are you eating?" she asked the dog. "What have you got in your mouth?"

She prised the dog's teeth apart and pulled out a used tissue.

"Yuck. The dog eats any sick thing that's on the floor," Alesha groaned.

"That's why you shouldn't drop things on the floor," Mum scolded.

Scruffy eats a used tissue, and *we* have to get a lecture!

"Remember last Halloween?" Mum continued, tossing the tissue wad into the waste-paper basket. "You left your trick-or-treat sweets on the floor —"

"And the stupid dog ate almost all of them!" I groaned.

"The poor thing was sick for a week," Mum said, petting his little brown head.

"Don't worry. I won't do that again!" I exclaimed.

Alesha finished her costume by taping a cardboard TV screen to the front of her sweat-shirt. Then we picked up our trick-or-treat bags and made our way to the front door.

Scruffy came running along with us. He thought he was going too.

"Don't stay out too late," Mum called from the hall. "And don't go too far from the neighbour-hood."

"Don't, don't, don't," I murmured. "Why is it

that parents like to take all the fun out of Halloween? What is their problem?"

"I guess they're scared," Alesha replied.

"What's to be scared about?" I asked.

Alesha didn't reply. Her funnel was tilting. She shoved it back up on her hair.

"I should talk baby talk all night since I'm a Teletubby," she said.

"What do you usually talk?" I cracked.

She shoved me off the front doorstep.

I got tangled in my cape and landed on my back in the grass.

"Great start," I muttered. I jumped up and pretended to stab her with my plastic sword.

It was a clear, cold night. A light frost made the front lawn shimmer.

I raised my eyes to the sky. "A full moon! Hey, Alesha — a full moon on Halloween! *Full Moon Fever!*"

She grinned. And opened her mouth to say something.

But we both gasped as we saw the big, ugly creature come staggering across our front garden.

Half-human, half-beast, it lurched forward, arms raised to the full moon. And it moaned, *"Help me . . . help me!"*

Alesha let out a scream — and ducked away as the beast made a grab for her.

I jumped aside too. And started to laugh when I realized we were staring at a big, furry Halloween costume.

With a grunt, the creature spun away from Alesha and dived towards me.

I reached out, grabbed the long, furry snout of the mask — and pulled the mask off.

"Maggie!" Alesha exclaimed.

We both stared at Alesha's best friend, Maggie Brown. Maggie reached out a furry paw and snatched the mask from my hands. "Grrrrr!" She growled at me and raked a paw in the air as if clawing me.

"Awesome costume!" Alesha exclaimed.

"You're supposed to be Barbie?" I joked.

"No. I'm *you*, Robbie!" Maggie shot back. She held out her arm. "It's real fur."

She uttered another growl. "I always wanted to be a wolf. Ever since I did that report on wolf packs last year. I just think they're so cool."

"Is it wolf fur?" Alesha asked, rubbing the furry costume sleeve.

"I don't know what fur it is," Maggie confessed.

"Probably baby seal," I joked.

"Shut up, Robbie!" Maggie cried. "That's not funny. That's sick."

I could hear Scruffy barking in the house. He'd probably seen Maggie through the window and thought she was a big dog.

"Are we going to get some sweets tonight or what?" I demanded impatiently. I swung my sword in the air. "If we don't get going, all the good stuff will be taken."

Maggie pulled her wolf mask down over her head. "I'm ready."

Alesha tilted her funnel up into place and straightened the cardboard TV screen on her belly. "Let's go."

"We'll go that way first," I said, pointing with my sword. "Then we'll come back on the other side of the street."

"I hope no one gives apples," Maggie said, her voice muffled beneath the heavy fur mask. "I hate it when they give apples, don't you?"

"What I hate are the acid drops," I replied. "I don't get it. Why does anyone like sweets that taste like lemons and make your mouth pucker up?"

We talked about sweets all the way down the block. The first house gave little Hershey bars. The second gave bags of candy corn. The third gave big Milky Ways.

We were off to a pretty good start.

After nearly an hour of going house to house, our trick-or-treat bags were bulging.

"Let's go home and pig out!" Alesha suggested. "I'm suddenly starving!"

"Me too," Maggie agreed.

But I had my eye on one more house.

The girls turned and saw me gazing at the dark, beat-up, broken-down house on the corner, half-hidden behind a tangle of trees. "Let's try that house," I said, starting across the street.

Alesha grabbed my arm and held me back. "Robbie — no," she pleaded. "That's Mrs Eakins's house."

"I know." I pulled my arm free. "Come on. Let's see what she's handing out."

"No. Please —" Alesha begged. "Please, Robbie. You *know* we can't go there!"

"Mrs Eakins hates us!" Alesha cried. "Remember when you kicked that soccer ball through her front window? She screamed at us like a lunatic. She threatened to call the police."

"And she wouldn't give me my ball back," I added, shaking my head.

"We can't trick-or-treat there. She *hates* us!" Alesha repeated, tugging my arm.

"We're in costume. She won't recognize us," I insisted. "Come on. Let's knock on her door. What can happen? I just want to see what kind of sweets she gives out."

"No way, Robbie!" Maggie declared. She pulled off her wolf mask. Her face was sweaty, and her hair was matted wetly against her forehead. "I'm not going near that house. That woman is crazy. And she might be dangerous. Everyone says she's a witch!"

I laughed. "Yeah, right. She's probably out riding around on a broomstick."

"It's true!" Maggie replied shrilly. "She cast a spell on Mrs Tarver across the street, and now Mrs Tarver can't stop blinking her eyes."

Alesha tugged my arm again. "Come on. Let's go home. Let's check out our sweets."

"One more house," I insisted. I pulled free of Alesha's grip. "Come on. It's Halloween. It's supposed to be a scary night." I started jogging up Mrs Eakins's front lawn.

"I'm outta here," Maggie called. "Really. I'm done. Catch you two later — if you survive!"

She took off, running down the pavement towards her house, her bag of sweets in one hand, the wolf head tucked under her arm. I had to laugh. Maggie's long furry wolf tail wagged to and fro as she ran.

"What a wimp," I muttered to Alesha.

My sister frowned at me. "She's not a wimp, Robbie. She's smart. It's late and we've been collecting sweets for an hour. Why should we —?"

I didn't wait for Alesha to finish. I jogged the rest of the way over the tall grass and weeds and leaped on to Mrs Eakins's front doorstep.

A big pumpkin rested against the wall of the house. A wreath of corn-cobs hung on the door. Dim light escaped from a tiny window at the top of the front door.

"Robbie — she *hates* us!" Alesha repeated in a whisper. She stood behind me at the bottom of the doorstep. The cardboard TV screen had fallen off the front of her costume. The funnel on top of her head tilted to the left.

"That was *weeks* ago, Alesha. She won't even remember us."

I pressed the doorbell.

I didn't hear it ring inside the house. So I knocked loudly on the door.

After a few seconds, I heard footsteps inside.

I raised my sweets bag in front of me.

I heard a lock click. And then, slowly . . . very slowly . . . the front door swung open.

"Well, well. What have we here?"

Mrs Eakins pulled open the door and poked her head out from the dim light of her hallway.

She had a round face, smooth, not wrinkled like an old person's, big, dark eyes, and full red lips. Her long, wavy white hair was pulled straight back and tied behind her head with a black ribbon. She was dressed in black, a black pinafore over a black turtle-neck.

She raised pale, slender hands to the sides of her face as she inspected us. "And what are you two supposed to be?" she asked. "Ghouls or goblins?"

"I — I'm Zorro," I stammered. "And she —" I pointed to Alesha, still hanging back a little way behind me. "She's a Teletubby."

Mrs Eakins laughed, pressing her hands against her face. "I love Halloween!" she declared cheerily. "It's my favourite holiday."

I can't believe she's being so nice, I thought.

I suppose she really doesn't recognize Alesha and me.

I raised my bag. "Trick or treat," I said.

Her dark eyes studied me for a moment. She reached out and plucked a leaf off my cape.

"Yes. Yes. I can see you've been collecting a lot of sweets," she said, a smile spreading on her full red lips. "Let me see what I have for you."

She disappeared back into the house.

I turned to Alesha. "See?" I whispered. "I told you it would be okay."

Alesha had her eyes on the front door.

Still smiling, Mrs Eakins leaned out again. "Here you go, Zorro." She handed me two bars. She stepped on to the doorstep and leaned down to hand two bars to Alesha.

"Happy Halloween, kids!" Mrs Eakins declared. "I love your costumes. Very original."

She hurried back into the house. The door closed gently behind her. I heard the lock click. The dim light went out.

"See?" I repeated. I jumped down off the doorstep. "I told you not to be a wimp."

Alesha shrugged. "Okay, okay. Can we go home now? All these sweets are making me so hungry!"

"Fine. Let's go," I agreed. I tossed one of Mrs Eakins's bars into my bag. I peeled open the other bar and took a big bite of it.

Alesha did the same. We walked slowly to the street, chewing the chocolatey bar. Alesha pulled off her funnel and tossed it into her bag.

"Mmmm. That bar was excellent. I think I need at least six more!" she exclaimed. "What kind was it?"

I still had the torn wrapper in my hand. I spread it out between my fingers and struggled to read it in the moonlight. "It's a Best bar," I reported. I crumpled up the wrapper and tossed it into my bag.

"It really *is* the best!" Alesha declared. She rummaged in her bag. "I can't find the other one."

"We're almost home," I told her. We crossed the street. I saw a group of little trick-or-treaters dancing and jumping excitedly up someone's driveway.

"Alesha, since you like it so much, I'll trade you my other Best bar."

"Trade it for what?" she asked suspiciously.

"For two Crunch bars."

"No way," she snapped. "One for one. I'm not giving you two, Robbie." She kicked my bag. "You're so greedy, you're sick!"

Sick.

The word reminded me of something.

I stopped and gazed up at the moon. A full moon.

A full moon on Halloween.

32

"Full Moon Fever," I murmured.

Alesha was rummaging in her bag again. She pulled out a pack of candy corn, tore it open, and began shovelling the sweets into her mouth. "Huh? What did you say?"

"Full Moon Fever," I repeated. I flashed her a devilish grin. "Come on. Let's see if the story is true."

We reached our corner. I put my bag down on the pavement. Then I pulled off my mask and dropped it into the bag.

"You're crazy," she replied, chewing hard. "I'm not doing it."

"Give me a break, Alesha. Why do you have to argue about everything?" I demanded impatiently.

"Why do you have to be so crazy?" she shot back. "First you have to knock on that old woman's door. Now you want to stop and stare up at the full moon."

"I just want to have some fun," I explained. "You know. Do something a little bit exciting. A little bit daring."

She scowled at me. "Well, maybe I don't *want* a case of Full Moon Fever!"

I laughed. "So you *believe* Grandpa John's story! You think it's true!"

"I do not!" she insisted. "I think it's stupid. That's all. I just want to go home and get out of the cold and pig out on sweets."

"It will only take a second," I said. I didn't give her a chance to cross the street. I grabbed the trick-or-treat bag from her hand. Then I jumped in front of her to block her path.

"One second. Two seconds maybe," I said. "Then we'll go home."

Alesha sighed. "This is so stupid." Her shoulders slumped. "What do you want me to do?"

"Nothing. Just stand here," I replied.

I turned her until she faced the moon. Then I stepped close beside her.

"Just look up," I instructed.

"This is soooooo lame," she wailed. But she obeyed.

We both tilted our heads back and gazed up at the full moon, so low and bright in the sky.

We didn't talk. We didn't move.

One second. Two. Three. . .

And then my whole body shuddered violently as a powerful wave of white light — so cold . . . so freezing cold — washed over me.

I felt a strong jolt. As if I'd been shocked by electricity.

As if I'd been struck by lightning.

The white light closed round me.

So bright. I couldn't see. I couldn't move.

"Noooooo!" Somewhere outside the light, I heard Alesha scream.

I opened my mouth to call to her. But I couldn't make a sound.

The light slowly began to fade.

I realized I was sweating. Cold drops of sweat rolled down my face. My shirt clung wetly to my back.

Darker.

The houses, the street, the trees came back into view.

My body trembled. My teeth chattered. Sweat rolled down my face, prickled the back of my neck.

"Alesha —" I managed to choke out her name.

But then I felt so sick.

My stomach tightened, tightened into a tiny, hard ball, as if someone was squeezing me. Squeezing me so hard, I couldn't breathe.

"So sick. . ." I murmured, dropping to my knees. "I feel so weak . . . so sick. . ."

I started to collapse.

The ground tilted — and roared up to meet me.

I felt the hard, cold concrete slap my forehead.

Then everything went black.

I blinked. Once. Twice.

Forced myself to wake up.

Tried to lift my head. Blinked again. Blinked into bright light.

Sunlight?

Where am I?

I was lying flat on my back, staring at a window. Dark curtains at the sides. Orange sunlight reflecting off the window glass.

Morning sunlight.

I tested my muscles. Tried to move. Stretched my arms up until they bumped the headboard behind me.

I'm in bed.

I'm in my *own* bed, I realized.

I'm home. And it's morning. And I'm lying in my own bed. Safe. Perfectly safe and okay.

It was a dream, I realized.

All a frightening dream.

I sighed as I gazed at the beautiful sunlight.

I wanted to laugh. I wanted to cheer.

All a dream. . .

Breathing hard, I started to sit up.

And gazed down at my bedclothes.

And opened my mouth in a shrill scream of horror.

The blanket. The sheets. They were shredded.

Clawed and torn. Clawed to bits.

"Nooo —" I choked out in a hoarse rasp.

Uttering low grunts, I jumped out of bed. And stared down at the shredded sheets and blankets.

At my pillow, covered in — *what*?

Covered in short, straight black hairs. Fur?

Black fur over my pillow. Over my sheets.

What has happened here?

What has HAPPENED?

My breath escaping in noisy, wheezing pants.

My eyes blinking in the harsh sunlight. Blinking at the horror of my bed. My room.

All wrong. Everything wrong.

What has HAPPENED?

Muddy footprints over the pale blue rug. Big footprints leading from the door to my bed.

Animal footprints.

Grunting, my chest heaving up and down.

38

Raspy breaths escaping my open mouth, I staggered across the bedroom to my mirror.

And stared at even more horror.

Stared wide-eyed at a monster.

I still had my straight black hair. But beneath it . . . a snout — a long wolf snout with wet black nostrils. I opened my jaws and saw two jagged rows of yellow animal teeth.

I raised my arms. Yes, I still had human arms, human hands. But the backs of my hands and arms were covered in thick, bristly black fur.

Short black fur tufted over the back of my neck and down my back.

My eyes — only my eyes were the same. My eyes. My bright blue eyes.

But everything else — monstrous and ugly.

Full Moon Fever!

It's true. It's all true.

Grandpa John didn't make it up.

Full Moon Fever. I have it, I realized.

Last night, I gazed up at the Halloween full moon. And the light swept down over me. And now I have it.

And Alesha?

Does Alesha have it too?

Grunting under my breath, my wet snout dripping, my beastly stomach growling, I lurched away from the mirror.

My feet, the tops covered in black fur, tripped

over the bedpost. I stumbled forward heavily, snarling.

Caught my balance on the edge of the bed. The bed all shredded, all torn.

My fur-covered arms brushed the door frame as I lumbered out into the hall.

Grunting and panting.

My teeth snapping together. My bare feet slapping the carpeted hall floor with my animal claws.

Down the hall, trailing one hand along the wallpaper.

I stopped in front of Alesha's door.

Does she have it too? Does she?

I raised a hairy fist — and pounded on her door.

I pounded again on Alesha's door. I heard a cracking sound and felt the door start to splinter.

I stared at my fist. My ugly, fur-covered fist that now had the strength of a beast.

Alesha. I tried to call my sister's name. But the word came out as a low grunt.

"*Annnnngggh.*"

"*Gohhhhh.*" She grunted on the other side of the door.

Oh, no.

I shut my eyes. Alesha had caught it too. Alesha had caught Full Moon Fever.

"*Let me in!*" I tried to call. But my fat tongue tangled in the jagged teeth of my new snout. The words came out: "Lllll meeeee!"

She didn't open the door.

"Gohhhhh wwwway!" I heard her animal wail. A terrified, painful wail.

"Nnnnooooooh!" I groaned.

I raised my fur-covered fist — and pushed the bedroom door in. It splintered as if it were made of paper. I stepped in, kicking the wood away with my big feet.

Alesha stood hunched in front of her mirror. Panting hard, she glared at me. Her bright blue eyes the same as always. Only her eyes. Everything else had changed.

She furiously swung her hairy fists above her head. And let out a roar, half-angry, half-crying.

Then, with a roar of rage, she flew at me. Threw herself at me. And began pounding my furry chest with both fists.

All my fault.

I knew what she was saying. This was all my fault.

But how was I to know that Grandpa John's story was true? How could I know that Full Moon Fever was real? Grandpa John told us he'd made it up!

We wrestled across the floor. She pounded me angrily with both fists, growling, snapping her jagged teeth.

I tried to push her away.

But she ducked — grabbed me — and heaved me into the wall.

I uttered a startled cry. Then I hurtled myself forward and tackled her with both arms.

We struggled some more, wrestling like wild animals round the room.

Her bedside table toppled over. Hit the floor on its side with a loud crash.

The sound made us both stop fighting.

I stood hunched over, paws on my knees, my chest heaving, struggling to catch my breath.

"Whhhhaaat dooooo?" Alesha demanded breathlessly.

What are we going to do? I wondered too.

I shook my head.

"Mummmmmm!" Alesha growled.

Yes. We had to tell Mum and Dad. What else could we do?

Somehow we had to explain what had happened to us.

Somehow we had to get them to help us.

I led the way out of Alesha's room. We stepped over the broken door and into the hall.

We lumbered down the stairs, grunting under our breath.

Wheezing loudly, pulling our monstrous bodies over the floor, we made our way to the kitchen.

"Mummmmmmm!" I cried, seeing her at the sink. "Mummmmm!"

43

Mum wheeled round.

Her eyes bulged with horror.

She dropped the coffee cup she was holding. It crashed to the floor and shattered. A puddle of brown coffee spread at her feet.

"Wh-what *are* you?" she stammered.

"Mummmmm — meeeee!" I tried to explain, waving my furry arms wildly in front of me. But I couldn't control my tongue, my teeth, my breath. My words came out in a harsh, animal growl.

Mum opened her mouth in a shriek of panic. Her whole body shuddered. "Get *away*!" she screamed, trembling, tearing at the sides of her hair. "Are you *monsters*? Are you *animals*? Get *out* of here!"

She backed against the worktop. She grabbed a broom. She swung it at Alesha and me.

"Get *out*! Get *out*!"

She swung the broom at us again and began

to scream for help at the top of her lungs. "*Monsters! Somebody — HELP! Monsters!*"

"Mummmmmm!"

I had to explain. I had to show her that it was Alesha and me. I had to tell her about Full Moon Fever.

"It's us — Alesha and Robbie!" I wanted to say. "Don't be afraid! We're not wild animals! You have to save us!"

But I couldn't get the words out. And her screams hurt my ears. Made my head throb.

She swung the broom hard, and it swiped across my stomach.

"AAAARRRRGH!" A furious roar of rage burst from my chest.

I grabbed the broom — ripped it from her hands. And broke it in half over my knee.

Beside me, Alesha swept her furry hand over the breakfast table. She sent all the bowls and glasses clattering to the floor. Then she began tossing plates against the wall.

We can't control our anger! I realized.

We really are *beasts*!

Mum stopped screaming. She gaped at us, trembling, hands gripping the worktop edge tightly, her mouth hanging open in horror.

"Please —" she choked out in a whisper.

Alesha shoved her fist through a glass cabinet door. The glass cracked and shattered.

"Mum — help us!" I wanted to cry out. "We

45

can't control ourselves. We don't want to wreck everything. But we can't help it!"

Instead, another loud roar burst from my long snout.

Mum edged along the worktop, her eyes on us. "Please —" she uttered again. "Please — go away."

And then she dived towards the wall. Grabbed the phone. Pushed three buttons.

"Police!" she cried into the receiver. "Get me the police! Hurry!"

A wave of anger tore through me. I moved quickly across the kitchen. I saw everything in a blur of angry red.

I grabbed the phone in both hands — and ripped it off the wall.

Mum screamed and stumbled back.

I heaved the phone into the hall.

Out of control. I'm out of control. . .

I felt only rage. Red-hot rage that made my muscles tighten, that made me grit my jagged teeth and growl.

My anger controlled my brain, I realized.

I stood in the centre of the room, my chest heaving up and down, wheezing breathlessly.

Alesha had the refrigerator open. She was trying to rip the door off!

We have to get away from here, I decided.

Wrecking the kitchen is bad enough. But

what if we do something *really* horrible? What if we hurt Mum?

I couldn't let that happen.

I stumbled across the kitchen. I grabbed Alesha's furry arm and tugged her away from the refrigerator.

Alesha pulled back, flashing me an angry, suspicious stare.

But I dragged her to the kitchen door.

A few seconds later, we were running across the back garden. My body felt so heavy. I couldn't stand up straight. I ran hunched over, my arms practically dragging along the ground.

My stomach growled. I felt a powerful pang of hunger.

It had been sunny. But now dark rain clouds floated low overhead. The cold air felt good against my hot face.

And it felt good to run.

Running side by side, grunting and huffing, Alesha and I made our way through gardens. We tried to stay out of sight, hunching behind fences and hedges as we ran.

Where were we going? What were we going to do?

I had no idea. I couldn't think clearly. I couldn't make a plan.

I saw everything through a thick red haze.

We scrambled over a carpet of dead autumn

47

leaves. Tore through a clump of shrubs. Ran across a street into another back garden.

A few houses down the block, I saw a group of kids walking to school.

I listened for their screams of horror. But I suppose they didn't see Alesha and me.

Didn't see the two furry half-beasts stampeding wildly, running, running because we were animals and we didn't know what else to do.

And then, as we ran, the hunger took over.

My stomach growled and then churned.

The hunger grabbed me. I couldn't think of anything else.

I had to eat. Had to eat. . .

I slowed to a walk. Beside me, Alesha slowed too. Her tongue lapped at the sides of her snout.

My eyes swept the ground. Through the red haze, I saw a shadow at the base of a tree.

And then the shadow came into sharper focus. A squirrel.

I didn't think. Some kind of animal instinct took charge.

I plunged across the ground.

I grabbed the squirrel in both hands before it could move.

My hands wrapped tightly round its plump, furry body.

I could feel it tremble as I raised it to my open snout.

"Unnnnh!"

I let out a groan as Alesha pounced on to my back. She grabbed for the squirrel, snapping her jaws hungrily.

"We'll share it! *Share* it!" I tried to tell her.

But she pulled the quivering creature from my hands and jammed its belly into her mouth.

"Ohhhhhh." I groaned, hungry and sick at the same time.

What are we *doing*? I asked myself.

We're eating a *live squirrel*!

We've got to get help. But how?

We felt a little calmer after eating two squirrels.

I dug a hole in the dirt with my hands and buried the little squirrel bones.

Alesha and I licked our lips and our long, jagged teeth.

We tried talking to each other. We were both desperate to make a plan.

As we talked, we gained better control of our new snouts. We learned how to force less air through our vocal cords so that we didn't roar every time.

I repeated my name over and over, until I could say it clearly with my new tongue and teeth.

We hid behind a tall hedge. And we tried to think clearly.

"Grandpa Johnnnnnn can help us," I said. "He's the only one who knows about Full Moon Feverrrrrrr."

"Do you think he knows a cuuuuuuure?" Alesha asked, tilting her head thoughtfully.

"Heeeeee's our only hope," I murmured. I scratched my furry head. "But how do we get there?"

Grandpa John lived in the next town, nearly an hour's car ride away.

Alesha tilted her head to the other side, thinking. "Maaaaaaggie," she uttered finally.

I narrowed my eyes at her. "Maggie? Maaa-aaaggie doesn't drive."

"But her brother Claaaaay — heeee drives."

Yes. That's right. Maggie's brother Clay was eighteen. He had his own car. Maybe Maggie could convince Clay to drive us to Grandpa John's.

It was worth a try.

Keeping out of sight, Alesha and I ducked low behind shrubs and hedges and fences as we made our way down the block to Maggie's house.

Burrs and dead leaves clung to my fur as I ran. But I ignored them. I was thinking hard, about Maggie, about Clay, about Grandpa John.

We were panting hard by the time we reached Maggie's house. I felt my stomach start to churn with hunger again.

How many squirrels would I have to eat to feel full?

I let out an angry growl as I saw the car back down the driveway. I could see Maggie and her dad in the front.

He was driving her to school.

Alesha and I had just missed her.

"We'll run to schooooool and catch her there!" I cried.

Alesha shook her head and held me back. "No waaaaay. We can't go to school. Kids will seeeeee us. We'll frighten everyone."

I pulled away from Alesha. I knew she was right. But I could feel a knot of anger tightening my chest.

How could this be happening to us?

We're normal kids — not monsters, I thought unhappily.

If only I hadn't been so stupid. If only I hadn't forced Alesha to gaze up at the full moon with me. . .

"We'll wait outside schooool," I told her. "When Maaaaggie comes out, we'll talk to herrrrr."

Alesha agreed with the plan. "There are lots of houses opposite the schoooool," she said, plucking a fly from her fur. She popped it into her mouth. "We can hide in someone's gaaarden while we wait for school to be over."

A few minutes later, we hid in a front garden across the street from our school. I pressed myself flat against the broad trunk of an old maple tree. Alesha hunkered low behind an evergreen bush.

We watched kids arriving at school. Happy, normal kids. A lot of them were probably talking about Halloween, about what a great time they had, about all the sweets they collected last night.

Sweets. . .

My stomach gnawed. I needed to eat.

I dropped to my furry knees in the grass. Bending low, I dug with my fingers, scooping out little holes until I found brown-and-purple earthworms wriggling in the dirt.

Grunting happily, I began pulling up worms one by one and dropping them into my open mouth. I loved the way they felt, so warm as they wriggled on my tongue. One bite and they slid easily down my throat.

"We're not safe heeeere," Alesha grunted.

I glanced up and saw that she had been eating too. She had several fat black insects stuck to her teeth.

"Someone will seeeee us," she insisted. "We have a long time to wait. Let's hide in the back gaaarden."

Hunching low, I loped on all fours as I followed my sister round the side of the house to the back. I didn't see any lights in any of the windows. I hoped whoever lived here was away.

The garden was cluttered with kids' toys and

bikes and outdoor furniture that hadn't been put away. I saw a small white tool shed at the back fence.

Alesha and I made our way round the side of the white shingled garage. I stumbled over a lawn rake and went sprawling into the garage wall with a heavy *THUD*.

"Rrrowwwwr!" An angry growl escaped my throat. My head throbbed from where it hit the shingles.

I felt a furious tidal wave of anger shoot up my body.

With another roar, I grabbed a plastic kids' bike off the ground and crushed it between my hands.

So goooood. . . It felt so good.

I turned and ripped a shingle off the side of the garage. I heaved it over the back fence. Then, breathing hard, my heart thudding, I ripped off a few more shingles and tossed them as far as I could.

"I'm a monnnnnster!" I bellowed. I smashed my fist through the garage window. The shatter of glass was like music to me.

I turned and saw Alesha signalling to me with both hands, trying to get me to shut up.

"But I'm a monnnnnster!" I wailed again.

"Robbie — nooo!" my sister warned.

Too late.

The kitchen door swung open.

A big, middle-aged man in khakis, a plaid shirt, and hunting boots came running out. He had a furious scowl on his angry red face. "Hey!" he shouted. "Hey — hey — hey!"

I turned from the garage and growled at him. "Hey — hey —"

The man froze. His mouth hung open. He made a loud gulping sound.

His eyes darted frantically from Alesha to me.

"What —?" he gasped. "What *are* you?"

I turned to Alesha. My chest throbbed with anger. The anger pulsed in my eyes, bright red, so red I couldn't see.

"Get himmmm!" I growled. I leaped forward.

"Nooooo!" the man shrieked. "Help me — somebody!"

I dived at him, swiping my paws at his face.

He ducked to the side — and grabbed a garden rake off the ground. Waving the rake wildly, he stumbled forward.

And swung the metal claws furiously — into the side of Alesha's head.

"Hunnnh." She uttered a startled groan.

Her knees collapsed. Her eyeballs rolled up in her fur-covered head. She fell heavily to the grass.

"Please — please —" the terrified man begged. "Just go! Just *go*!"

"Aleeeesha — get up!" I moaned.

But she lay sprawled face down in the grass.
She didn't move.

"Please — go away! Go!" the man wailed.

Then he came charging at me. Swinging the
rake furiously. Swinging at my head.

I gazed down at my sister.

Then I prepared for a fight.

The man swung the rake at my head.

I ducked under the claws. Opened my mouth in a furious roar.

Diving forward, I swiped at him with both furry fists.

He dodged away. Lifted the rake. Started to swing it again.

The metal claws caught me in the side.

Knocked my breath out.

I staggered back against the garage wall.

With a groan, the man dived forward. Holding the rake in both hands, he pinned me to the garage with it. Pressed it with all his strength.

I'm trapped, I realized.

Alesha was still sprawled on the ground. Not moving. And now I was trapped.

Sweat poured down the man's forehead. He pushed the rake handle against my stomach.

Trapped . . . trapped. . .

I took a deep, wheezing breath. Then with a roar of power, I grabbed it — grabbed the rake with both hands.

He uttered a startled gasp.

I twisted the rake between my hands and snapped the handle in half.

Then I tossed the pieces against the side of the garage.

Shaking in terror, the man started to back away from me.

But I leaped into the air with another roar.

And sank my long, jagged teeth into the meaty part of his arm.

He opened his mouth in a howl of pain.

I let go, and he dropped to his knees. He grabbed his arm, trying to rub away the pain. Then he scrambled away, holding his arm.

I watched him until he vanished back into his house.

Grunting with each breath, my heart pounding, I bent down to my sister.

She stirred, uttered a soft groan. She opened her eyes.

"Robbie?" she murmured weakly. She raised her head. "Arrrre we — are we still *monsters*?"

I nodded. "Afraid so."

I helped her to her feet.

She shook her head hard. "I — I'm okay," she announced.

I heard the man's voice from inside the

house. I knew he must be phoning the police.

"We've got to get going," I told Alesha. I brushed some dead leaves from the fur on her shoulders. "We've got to hide somewhere else."

I took her hand and pulled her to the wooden fence at the back of the garden. The fence was high — way over our heads. But my legs seemed to have new strength.

With a loud grunt, I leaped — and grabbed the top. Alesha also jumped up easily.

We scrambled over the fence, into the next garden. Then we began to run hard, moving on all fours, grunting like animals, our heads bobbing as we ran.

We tore through a clump of shrubs. Made our way down a narrow alley, knocking over dustbins as we ran.

"Where are we goooooooing?" Alesha demanded without slowing down.

"Let's try to hide near Maggie's house," I suggested breathlessly.

The alley ended at a wide, two-way avenue. We burst into the street without stopping to look.

I heard the squeal of car tyres.

A woman screamed.

I heard the crash of glass and metal. More screams.

We didn't stop. We crossed into a small park, empty, the trees nearly bare.

I saw two robins poking at the hard ground. And felt a sharp pang of hunger. I pictured myself sinking my teeth into their soft orange chests.

But I kept running alongside Alesha.

Eat later, Robbie, I told myself. First, get to safety.

But where would we be safe?

People had seen us. The police would soon be out searching for us. Searching for two wild monsters.

Where could we hide?

We couldn't just wait in Maggie's back garden for her to get home from school. We couldn't be trusted. We were *animals*. We couldn't stop ourselves from destroying everything we saw.

We crossed another street. I heard the wail of sirens in the distance.

Maggie's redbrick house came into view. Alesha and I slowed to a stop.

The sirens were louder now. Closer.

Two workers in blue uniforms were up on Maggie's roof. I could see them working on the gutters.

"They'll see us!" I rasped. "We can't stay here."

"But where can we hiiiiide?" Alesha cried.

We both saw the manhole cover at the same time.

"The sewer!" I exclaimed.

Alesha let out a groan. "I don't *want* to wait in the sewer!"

The sirens grew louder.

From the house across the street, I heard a woman screaming.

"No choice," I murmured. Using my brand-new strength, I grabbed the heavy metal man-hole cover with both hands and slid it away from the sewer opening.

Grunting, Alesha lowered herself into the hole. I followed her in, then slid the cover back into place.

A sick, sour smell rose up to greet us.

We lowered ourselves into the damp, cold darkness.

"Will we be safe down here?" Alesha whispered.

I listened to the *PLUNK PLUNK PLUNK* of water dripping. And the high, chittering squeal of a sewer rat.

"Maybe," I replied.

15

Our eyes adjusted quickly to the darkness. We were standing on a narrow concrete ledge. Beneath the ledge, a shallow river of sewer water trickled past.

"I don't want to beeeee here," Alesha whispered, her furry back pressed against the concrete sewer wall.

I heard sirens overhead. Shouting voices.

"We have to stay here," I told her. "If we get caught before Maggie comes home. . ." My voice trailed off.

I felt another sharp pang of hunger.

I squatted down and leaned over the trickling sewer water, searching for something I could pluck out of the water and eat.

I found a few insects. But they tasted bitter and weren't at all filling.

Alesha was lucky. She found a long, fat worm floating near the surface. She said it tasted okay even though it had been dead for a long time.

After she swallowed the last of it, she turned to me sadly. "I don't want to beeee a monster," she uttered. She still had a few shreds of worm caught in her teeth.

"Maggie will help us," I promised. "She'll get us to Grandpa John. He'll know a cure for Full Moon Fever. I'm sure he will."

The sirens faded. The voices overhead were silent.

We hunkered against the sewer wall. We watched the thick, murky water flow past. We breathed in the putrid odours.

And we waited.

A little after three-thirty, I crawled up to the top of the sewer and shoved the cover aside. I blinked as late afternoon sunlight poured down on me.

Alesha and I pulled ourselves out of the sewer. We stood on the kerb and stretched our backs and furry arms. The air was cold, but the sunlight felt good on my face.

I kicked the metal cover back into place. The sour smell lingered on my skin and fur.

I turned to Maggie's house and saw that the roof workers had left. Down the block, two little kids climbed out of a car, home from school with their mother. A blue van turned on to the street and began rolling in our direction.

"Come on." I grabbed Alesha by the arm and dragged her off the street. "We've waited all day. We don't want to get caught now."

We scurried on to Maggie's front lawn and hid behind tree trunks.

"I hope Maggie comes straight hommmm-mme from school," Alesha murmured.

"I hope we can make her undersssstand us," I replied. "I hope we can make her believe us."

"She'll recognize us," Alesha said, licking her jagged teeth. "I'm her best friend. She'll recognize me. She won't be afraid."

At that moment, I saw Maggie turn the corner. She was walking slowly, her rucksack bouncing on her shoulders.

As she started up the driveway, Alesha saw her too.

"Maaaaaggie!" Alesha shrieked. Throwing out her arms, Alesha burst out from behind the tree and went running across the lawn to Maggie.

Maggie stopped.

Her mouth opened in horror.

The rucksack slid from her shoulders and thudded to the ground.

"Maaaaaaggie!" Alesha cried happily. "It's meeeee!"

Maggie let out a shrill scream of horror.

Then, still screaming, she turned and ran.

"Nooooooo!" Alesha howled in protest.

She chased after Maggie, howling and wheezing.

Maggie ran down the centre of the street. She waved both arms frantically, shouting for help.

I started after them. "Maggie — pleeeeease!" I cried. "Wait!"

But Maggie was shrieking too loudly to hear me.

Just before the corner, Alesha leaped into the air. She plunged over the tarmac — and tackled Maggie to the street.

"Let me go! Let me go!" Maggie wailed, kicking and thrashing.

"It's me! It's meeee!" Alesha rasped, struggling to stay on top of her, to keep Maggie pinned to the ground.

I jogged up to them breathlessly. "Maaaaggie — don't be afraid!" I cried. "It's ussss!"

"Please!" Maggie wailed, twisting and kicking. "Don't hurt me!"

"It's usssss!" I insisted. I leaned over her. "Maggie — look in my eyes. Look at Alesha's eyes. Our eyes are the same. It's us — Robbie and Alesha."

"Huh?" She stopped struggling, but her eyes stayed wide with fright. "Huh? Robbie?"

"My eyes," I repeated. "Look at my eyes. Don't you recognize me?"

"But —" Maggie gazed up at me, then at Alesha. She studied us for a long moment. Then her expression slowly changed. Her fear changed to confusion.

"It *is* you!" she declared weakly.

Alesha let go of her and climbed to her feet. She bent and helped pull Maggie off the tarmac.

"But how?" Maggie began. "I mean —"

"You've got to help us," I told her. I handed Maggie her rucksack. I brushed a clump of dirt off the back of her parka.

"It's really you?" she cried again, her eyes darting from Alesha to me. "What *happened*?"

"Full Moon Fever," Alesha replied. "We've got to get to Grandpa John's house. You've got to help us, Maaaaaggie."

"You — you're *monsters*!" Maggie stammered. She shook her head as if trying to shake the picture of us away. "Do you feel okay? Does it hurt? What is Full Moon Fever?"

"We don't have time to explain," Alesha said.

"We've got to change back to ourselves," I added.

The three of us started walking towards Maggie's house.

Maggie kept swallowing hard, shaking her head, gazing at us in disbelief.

"Will you help us?" Alesha demanded as we reached her front door.

I bumped into a big jack-o'-lantern on the doorstep, left over from Halloween.

"Huh? How can I help you?" Maggie demanded. "What can I do?"

We stepped inside. The house was warm. I could hear music playing somewhere upstairs.

"Your brother Clay," I said. "Is he at home? He can drive us. He can drive us to Grandpa John's house."

"Please —" Alesha begged, grabbing Maggie's arm.

Maggie gasped in fright and jerked her arm away.

"Please —" Alesha repeated. "Ask him. Ask him if he'll drive us. We've got to get to Grandpa John's."

Maggie hesitated. She swallowed again. "Okay," she finally agreed. "I'll see —"

"Thannnnk you!" Alesha cried.

She started to hug Maggie but pulled back, remembering how frightened Maggie was.

Something against the wall flashed in my eyes. I narrowed my eyes to focus on it.

The aquarium.

On the bookshelf against the wall, Maggie's parents had a big aquarium of fat orange-and-yellow goldfish.

My tongue dropped out from my long, toothy jaw.

I lumbered across the room to the lighted tank.

I watched the plump fish swim silently in the bubbling water.

I couldn't help it. I couldn't resist. I couldn't stop myself.

I plunged both hands into the tank.

I pulled out two big orange fish. One of them almost slipped free, but I tightened my hand round it.

And then I shoved both goldfish into my mouth. I bit down hard. They made a wonderful *SQUISH* sound.

I closed my eyes and chewed.

Mmmmmm.

So hungry. I didn't realize how hungry I was.

I opened my eyes. Turned and reached into the tank for more delicious fish.

Maggie's screams forced me to stop.

I turned to see her shoving Alesha to the door. "Get out! Get out of my house!" Maggie cried furiously. "Both of you — *get out of here!*"

The music upstairs stopped suddenly. I heard heavy footsteps thudding down the stairs. Clay?

Alesha and I turned and ran.

"Get out! Get out!" Maggie screamed.

We burst out on to the front doorstep. The door slammed behind us, but I could still hear Maggie shrieking inside.

I jumped off the doorstep.

But Alesha turned back to the house. She reached down and ripped off a big chunk of the jack-o'-lantern. She heaved it against the front door.

Then she dug her hand into the pumpkin again and pulled out a hunk of pumpkin meat. She jammed it hungrily into her mouth.

My stomach growled. I leaped back on to the doorstep. Dug into the pumpkin. I tore off a huge piece of the soft rind and gobbled it hungrily.

Then, with sticky, wet pumpkin smeared on our faces, Alesha and I took off, running.

Once again, we stayed out of view, away from the street, keeping low, behind shrubs and hedges, sometimes running on all fours.

After a few minutes, we stopped behind someone's garage to catch our breath.

"Maggie wanted to help us," Alesha said, sighing. "But then you had to gobble up her fish. . ."

"I couldn't help it," I replied, breathing hard from our long run. "I was so hungry, and they looked so good."

"We're *animals*!" Alesha wailed. "We're disgusting animals!"

I rubbed pumpkin off my face with both hands. "I know," I agreed sadly. "I *bit* that man with the rake. Can you belieeeeve it? I bit a man!"

"I ate dead worms from the sewer," Alesha said softly. And then she added, "And I actually *liked* them!"

"Yes. We're animals."

I shut my eyes and suddenly pictured Mum and Dad.

They must be so worried, I thought.

So worried and confused.

Mum thought she was attacked by two monsters this morning. And now she must think the monsters carried Alesha and me away or something.

Should we go home? I wondered. Should we go home and try to make Mum and Dad understand?

I turned to Alesha, and I could see she was thinking hard too.

"We have no choice," she said, shaking her head. "We have to *walk* to Grandpa John's. We have to get there, Robbie — as soon as possible. The longer we stay monsters. . ." Her voice trailed off.

"Okay. We'll wait until dark," I agreed. "Then we will walk there. We'll get there — if it takes all night."

It took most of the night. We followed the highway, walking in the tall grass along the shoulder. We had to duck low whenever a car passed.

We knew the police were probably looking for us. We couldn't let anyone see us.

After walking for more than three hours, we dived behind a tall shrub as a large van went by. It started to roar past, but then we heard the squeal of its brakes and saw it skidding to a stop.

"They saw us!" I whispered, dropping to the hard, cold ground. "We've been caught."

But to our relief, the van started up again and roared away.

"What was *that* about?" I growled. My heart still pounded in my fur-covered chest.

Alesha and I made our way closer to the road, and we saw why the van had skidded.

A hare lay flattened in the middle of the highway.

The hare must have run out on to the road. The driver of the van had hit the brakes and swerved. Too late.

I bent and picked up the dead hare in both hands. It was still warm.

I turned to Alesha. "Do you want white meat or dark?" I asked her.

The hare meat was sweet but a little chewy. I was so hungry, I could have eaten six more!

"I don't believe it. We're eating roadkill." Alesha groaned, sucking the last bit of leg meat off the bone.

"We're almost at Grandpa John's," I told her, starting to walk again. "Then this nightmare will be over."

It was nearly morning when we arrived at Grandpa John's cottage in the woods. A freezing morning dew had fallen. Alesha and I were shivering in the damp cold. The sky was still black as night.

He didn't have a doorbell, so we knocked on the wooden door.

Silence inside.

"It's so early. He must be asleep," Alesha said softly. She tugged nervously at the thick fur on the back of her neck.

73

"We'll wake him up," I said.

We both pounded on the door with our fists. I tilted back my head and let out a shrill animal howl.

Then we pounded some more.

After a long wait, the cottage door swung open.

Grandpa John stared out sleepily. He wore baggy red-and-white-striped pyjamas. His white hair was matted flat against his head.

"Ohh!" He uttered a startled cry and started to slam the door.

But I lowered my shoulder, pushed the door open, and shoved myself inside the cottage.

Grandpa John went stumbling back against the wall.

Alesha hurried inside and stepped up beside me. "Grandpa John — it's *us*!" she cried.

His eyes wide with terror, he pressed his back against the wall and raised both hands as if to shield himself.

"It's us — Robbie and Alesha!" I cried.

"Don't be sssscared!" Alesha hissed.

"But — but —" he sputtered. His face went nearly as red as his pyjamas.

"Grandpa John — listen to us!" I insisted. "We caught it. We caught Full Moon Fever."

"Huh?" He narrowed his eyes at us intently, studying me, then Alesha. "It *is* you!" he

74

declared finally. A smile spread over his red face. "You're wearing Halloween costumes? Is that it? Those are costumes?"

"Listen to us!" I insisted. "They're not costumes. We're monsters! Monsters!"

"It's Full Moon Fever!" Alesha declared heatedly.

"No!" Grandpa John gasped, shaking his head. "No — it can't be! That was just a story! Just a wild story! It's not true!"

"LOOK AT US!" I roared. "It's TRUE! We caught it!"

His eyes bulged, but he didn't reply. He stared at us in confused silence.

Then he reached out a trembling hand and grabbed my arm. He tugged at the thick brown fur on my arm. Tugged it hard.

"Real," he murmured.

"Yes," I said, nodding sadly. "You're the only one who can help us."

"You've got to cure us!" Alesha insisted. "You've got to cure us — now!"

"But — but I can't," Grandpa John stammered. "Don't you understand? There *is* no cure for Full Moon Fever."

"Noooo!" I cried, shaking my fists at him. "There *has* to be a cure!"

"Why did you say that?" Alesha growled at Grandpa John.

Grandpa John shrugged his slender shoulders. "How can there be a cure when there is no such disease?" he cried. "Full Moon Fever — it's just a crazy story! It's just —"

He stopped. He blinked his eyes. He swept a hand back through his long, stringy white hair. "Wait," he murmured.

"Huh? What do you mean?" I demanded.

Alesha lurched forward eagerly, nearly knocking him over. "Do you have an idea?"

Grandpa John nodded, thinking hard. "The old woman who told me the story. She did talk about a cure. She said the victim of Full Moon Fever must wait until the next full moon. Then he must stand under the moonlight once again and wait for the moment, the right moment."

Grandpa John's eyes flashed excitedly. "Yes. That's what you must do. Next month, when the full moon arrives —"

"We can't wait!" I shrieked. *"Don't you understand?"*

My chest felt ready to explode. I saw red — bright red. I couldn't control my anger.

With a furious roar, I dived across the room. I grabbed the side of Grandpa John's new armchair in both hands — and ripped the arm off the chair.

Then, with animal strength, I heaved the heavy leather arm at the cottage window. It shattered the glass and sailed out into the darkness.

Alesha tilted her head back in an excited roar.

"Weeeeee can't waaaaait!" I growled.

Grandpa John tried to back up and stumbled over the sofa. He fell back on the cushion and stayed there. His eyes were wide with fright. He had his skinny grasshopper arms raised in front of him like a shield.

"Don't you understand?" Alesha cried, panting, the fur rising up and down on her back. "We're *monsters*! We kill things and eat them!"

"I *bit* a man!" I growled at Grandpa John. "I *bit* a man today! And it tasted *good*! What will I do next time? I'm a monster! What will I do?"

"The police are searching for us," Alesha

continued. "If they catch us, we'll *never* get cured."

Alesha and I leaned over the sofa, leaned over Grandpa John, snapping our animal jaws, drool running from our mouths as we roared at him.

"We can't wait till the next full moon," I growled.

"You've got to help us now!" Alesha told him.

I felt a sharp pang of hunger.

"But — but — what can I do?" Grandpa John sputtered. He remained sprawled helplessly on his back.

Alesha and I leaned over him, grunting, breathing hard.

Alesha turned to me.

I stared back at her.

And at that moment, I think we both realized that we were going to *eat Grandpa John!*

"Noooooo!"

With another furious howl, I forced myself back to the wall.

What a thought! What a horrible thought!

Control yourself, Robbie! I ordered myself. I shut my eyes and concentrated. *Control yourself!*

Alesha was still leaning over Grandpa John hungrily, licking her jagged rows of teeth.

With a frightened cry, Grandpa John squirmed out from under her and climbed to his feet. His eyes bulging with fear, he turned from Alesha to me.

Suddenly, I had an idea. "Take usssss to the old woman," I told him.

"Yesssss!" Alesha hissed. "The old woman in the north woods. The woman who told you the story of Full Moon Fever. Take us to her."

"She was real — wasn't she?" I demanded. "She wasn't part of the story?"

Grandpa John nodded. "She was real," he

murmured. "But — but —" He tore tensely at his white hair.

"But what?" I growled.

"What if she isn't there any more? What if I can't find her?" Grandpa John sputtered. "What if she doesn't know any other cure for Full Moon Fever?"

Alesha and I replied in unison: "We have to try. . ."

Alesha and I pulled all the meat out of Grandpa John's freezer. We sat on the floor, breaking off frozen chunks and gobbling them.

While we ate, Grandpa John made phone calls.

First he called our parents and told them where we were. Mum and Dad were worried and upset. Grandpa John told them we were fine and that he'd bring us home in a few days. "I'll explain everything then," he promised.

Then he called the airlines and made plane reservations. Then he made several calls until he found a travel agents that was open.

Alesha and I grunted and growled as we stuffed ourselves with the frozen meat. The cold chunks crunched as we ground them down between our sharp animal teeth.

I looked up to see Grandpa John heading out of the door. "What's up?" I called, spitting a big gob of meat on to the floor.

"Be back in less than an hour," Grandpa John replied. He disappeared out of the door. A few seconds later, we heard him start up his van and drive away.

Alesha and I went back to our pile of frozen meat.

We didn't learn why Grandpa John went out until we arrived at the airport the next morning. Then he pulled two long grey plastic cases from the back of the van.

"Cargo carriers," he explained.

He pulled open the lids on the two boxes. "Climb in. You two have to travel as cargo."

"Whoooaa —" I hesitated.

"You can't travel as passengers," he explained. "They won't let you on the plane. You have to travel in the cargo hold. It's the only way."

"But how will we breathe?" Alesha demanded.

Grandpa John pointed to the sides of the long cases. "Air holes. See? Dozens of air holes. On the top too. You'll breathe okay. Hurry. If anyone sees you. . ."

Alesha and I had no choice.

We lowered our furry bodies into the cases. Grandpa John closed the lids over us. We heard him snapping the locks.

I was panting hard. I wanted to roar and

shove my fists against the lid. I didn't like being locked up like an animal.

A few minutes later, I heard voices and felt the case being hoisted off the ground. Through the air holes, I could see several uniformed men lifting the cases on to a cart.

"Ooooof." I felt a hard bump as Alesha's case was dropped on top of mine.

Then we were moving. Rolling on to the runways behind the airport terminal.

I could see an enormous jet plane. At its nose stood a long line of cargo, crates, boxes and suitcases. Alesha and I were dumped alongside them.

I peered out. Men were hoisting the crates and boxes on to a conveyor belt. The conveyor belt led up to the cargo hold of the plane.

We're okay, I told myself, breathing a sigh of relief. No one has spotted us. In a short while, we'll be in the plane, on our way to finding a cure.

I watched the boxes and suitcases roll up the conveyor belt and disappear into the open cargo hatch.

Through the air holes, I saw the workers move towards our cargo cases. Two men stooped to reach for my case.

I tightened my muscles, prepared to be lifted.

But then, cold dread swept down my body as I heard a man shout: "No! Stop! Not those two! Don't take those two!"

20

The two uniformed men let go of my case. They spun round to face the man who was shouting at them.

"Not those two boxes," the man instructed. He pointed to two wooden crates piled next to us.

"They have to go back to the terminal. Just leave them there till you finish loading the rest."

Whew.

Close call.

A short while later, Alesha and I were lifted into the cargo hatch. My case was tossed down with a hard *THUD*. I covered my mouth to keep from crying out.

I heard another *THUD* and saw that Alesha was right beside me.

It was dark in the cargo hold and very cold. Dogs in their travel crates cried and barked.

The sound made me hungry.

I could go for a tasty dog right now, I thought, feeling my stomach grumble.

I imagined the soft fur against my tongue, the warm meat sliding down my throat.

I pressed my hands against the lid of the case. Could I break out? Could I push open the lid, creep out, and help myself to a dog or two?

Mmmmmm. . .

Their howls and barks were driving me crazy.

"Robbie — don't do it!" Alesha's voice echoed in the big cargo hold.

I laughed. "You read my mind!"

"I'm hungry too," Alesha growled. "But if we eat the dogs here, we might get caught."

I opened my mouth in a roar. "If they'd only shut up!" I cried.

The barking stopped. The dogs were whimpering now, frightened by my ferocious roar.

"Robbie?" Alesha's voice sounded tiny now. I peered through the air holes, but I couldn't see inside her case.

"Yes?" I called.

"Robbie — are you frightened?" she asked. "I am. I'm really frightened."

I was scared too. More scared than I'd ever been in my life. But I decided not to admit it.

"We'll be okay," I replied instead. "No problem, Alesha. We'll be fine."

*

"We're lost." Grandpa John sighed. "We're totally lost."

We had driven from the little airport in the Jeep Grandpa John had rented. Then for more than an hour we followed the narrow road that curved through the north woods.

The sun was setting behind the trees as the road became a dirt path. We bumped over the path until it ended suddenly at a thick wall of pine trees.

And then we had no choice. We had to climb out, leave the Jeep behind, carry all our supplies, and walk.

The grey sky turned to purple, then darkened to black. The air felt cold and damp. No moon or stars overhead to light our way.

Grandpa John's torch danced over the path ahead of us, bouncing off trees and jutting rocks. "I remember walking here," he kept repeating. "Yes. Yes. I remember that odd-shaped rock cliff. I'm sure we're on the right path, the path that leads to the old woman's cabin."

But after a while, he wasn't so sure.

Alesha and I made him stop a few times. He had to wait while my sister and I hunted down squirrels and badgers and plump raccoons and hungrily devoured them.

Then we walked through the darkening woods, our feet crunching over a thick carpet of dead leaves and pine needles.

86

We stopped in a small, round, grassy clearing. Grandpa John tugged at his white hair. He shifted his pack on his shoulders and glanced round. "I think we're lost," he murmured.

Birds hooted in the trees. Leaves rustled and cracked as small night creatures scampered over them.

"There should be another path," Grandpa John whispered, shaking his head. "I'm completely disorientated."

"Maybe we should camp out here overnight," Alesha suggested. "In the morning, we can see better. We can —"

"Wait!" I interrupted. "Check that out. Am I seeing things?"

I pointed to a tiny glow of orange light, half hidden between the trees.

"Is that a fire?" Alesha whispered.

It flickered dimly. "It could be," I murmured.

"Let's go and see," Grandpa John replied.

We ran across the clearing, into the trees. As we drew closer, a small cabin came into view. Orange firelight made the single tiny window glow.

"Is this the old woman's cabin?" I demanded, jogging between Alesha and Grandpa John.

He scratched his head. "I don't know. I'm not sure. It may be the same cabin. I really can't remember."

I shielded my eyes with one hand and

pressed my furry forehead against the window. The glass felt warm. I peered inside, waiting for my eyes to adjust to the light.

"I — I can't see anyone," I stammered.

"Someone has to be at home," Grandpa John said. "If there's a fire going. . ."

"Only one way to find out," Alesha declared. She stomped up to the front door, raised her fist, and pounded several times.

Silence inside the cabin.

Alesha uttered an angry growl. She pounded harder, with both fists.

The thin wooden door started to splinter.

Alesha raised her fists again — and the door swung open.

A short white-haired woman in a dark-blue dressing-gown poked her head out. She raised an enormous hunting rifle in her hands, a rifle almost as tall as she was.

"*Go away!*" she shrieked. "*Go away now — or you'll be sorry!*"

Alesha uttered an angry growl.

The old woman raised the enormous rifle.

"Go away! Go away!"

"Please — we've come for your help," Grandpa John said softly.

The old woman turned the rifle on him. Her watery eyes were wide with fright. She stared at him for a long time, and then her expression softened.

"I — I remember you," she stammered.

She kept the hunting rifle at her chest. "Why did you come back?"

"We need help," Grandpa John repeated. "My two grandchildren. . ." He motioned to us. "You can see that they are in trouble."

The old woman lowered the rifle to the ground. She squinted hard at Alesha and me. As she stared, her face wrinkled like dried fruit.

She shuddered. Pulled her gown tighter.

Turned to Grandpa John. "I don't understand. What has happened to them?"

"Full Moon Fever," Grandpa John replied. He shifted the heavy pack on his shoulders. Despite the cold of the night, big drops of sweat dotted his forehead.

"They've caught Full Moon Fever."

The old woman still blocked the doorway, one hand holding the rifle by the barrel. "The story I told you?"

"It isn't a story," Grandpa John told her. "It's true. My grandchildren . . . they stared into the full moon on Halloween night."

"Impossible," the old woman scowled. "A story is a story."

"*Look at us!*" I snarled. "*These aren't costuuu-uuumes! This is reeeeeal furrrr!*"

Alesha raked the air with both furry hands.

The old woman uttered a frightened squeak. She gripped the rifle barrel tighter.

"Impossible," she repeated, shaking her head, her white hair falling over the collar of her blue gown.

Her watery eyes locked on Grandpa John. "Why did you come back here with this crazy story? What do you expect me to do?"

"Can you help them?" Grandpa John asked. "Is there a cure for Full Moon Fever?"

"How should I know?" the old woman

snapped. "How should I know a cure for a disease that doesn't exist?"

Alesha and I exchanged glances. It's hopeless, I realized. My sister and I are trapped in these monstrous bodies. No one can help us.

And then the old woman's hoarse voice interrupted my unhappy thoughts. "There is one person in these woods who may be able to help you."

"*Whoooo?*" Alesha and I howled together.

Our animal cry made the old woman shudder again.

"You might try crazy old Dr Thorne," she replied. "Dr Thorne has lived in these woods for seventy years. Most people are afraid to go to him. He and his son — they're very strange. But he's your only hope. He was a real doctor when he was younger."

She rubbed her wrinkled cheek. "At least, that's what he tells everyone."

"How do we find Dr Thorne?" Grandpa John asked.

The old woman pointed with a trembling hand. "Follow the path. His house isn't far. Those of us who live in these woods try to stay close together."

Grandpa John bowed his head. "Thank you for your help. Sorry to disturb your sleep."

The old woman didn't reply. She closed the door hard. I heard her slide the bolt shut inside.

The three of us turned and made our way back to the path. A pale half-moon slid out from behind a cloud to light our way.

As we followed the path through the tall pine trees, I felt hopeful for the first time.

Maybe . . . maybe this old doctor will know a cure.

Maybe this nightmare will be over.

I had no way of knowing that the real horror was just beginning.

The old woman said that the doctor's house was near by. But we walked for a long time, at least an hour or two.

When we finally spotted the house, the moon was sinking behind the trees, and a ribbon of red morning sunlight spread over the horizon.

The house was long and low, built of bleached wood. As we came closer, it appeared to be a row of flat-roofed shacks boarded together.

"What is he doing with all those nets?" Grandpa John asked, pointing.

I saw several rope nets — fishermen's nets — stretched out on poles round the house. Another net stretched from the front of the house to the path.

"He can't use them for fishing," Grandpa John muttered. "There is no water round here for miles."

The house stood on a gentle slope, shaded

under tall pine trees. As we climbed the slope, I saw a bright red object in the tall grass.

A boat?

Before I could say anything about it, a chubby man with a mane of long red hair down past his shoulders, wearing overalls and a white sweatshirt, came bouncing down the hill to meet us.

"Are you Dr Thorne?" Grandpa John called.

The man laughed in reply. He swung his arms at his sides, his big belly bouncing as he walked.

He stopped short when he saw Alesha and me.

"Whoa!" he exclaimed. "What happened to you two?"

"Are you Dr Thorne?" Grandpa John repeated, wiping his forehead with the back of his hand.

The man shook his head. His blubbery chins shook with him. "No, sir. I'm Dr Thorne, *Junior*."

He couldn't stop staring at my sister and me. "Actually, my name is Roger. But everyone calls me Wolf."

"Wolf?" Grandpa John repeated. "Why do they call you Wolf?"

"Beats me." He laughed again.

I was standing next to the red boat. "Why do

you have a boat here in the middle of the woods?" I asked.

He stared at me a long time without replying. Finally, he motioned to the woods with a sweep of one hand. "Some day soon, this will all be water."

"Excuse me?" Alesha cried.

"The rains are going to come," he predicted, rubbing his many chins, a strange smile on his round face. "The woods will flood. This will be a raging river. And Dad and I will be ready for it."

He kicked the side of the boat. "We'll be the only ones who are ready," he declared.

He's crazy, I realized.

If his father is as crazy as he is, Alesha and I have no hope.

Without warning, Wolf reached out a chubby hand — and grabbed the thick fur on the back of my neck.

"Hey!" I cried out.

He let go quickly. His mouth dropped open in surprise. "It's real!" he exclaimed. He narrowed his small, round eyes at me. "Are you part *gorilla* or something?"

Alesha uttered an angry growl. As she stepped forward, I saw her entire body stiffen, preparing for a fight.

My stomach rumbled. It began to gnaw with hunger.

"I've never tasted *wolf* meat," I murmured, eyeing his chubby, round belly under the overalls.

Grandpa John stepped in front of Alesha and me. "These kids need your father's help right away," he told Wolf. "He is a doctor, right?"

"That's what he tells everyone," Wolf replied. His long red hair fluttered behind him in a strong breeze. The heavy nets all creaked and swayed in the sudden wind.

"The kids are in trouble," Grandpa John said solemnly. "Can we see the doctor now?"

Wolf chuckled for some strange reason. His little eyes flashed with amusement. "Follow me," he said, waving his chubby pink hand towards the house.

We followed him in through a side door. The house was low and narrow and dimly lit. A fire in a small fireplace had burned down to purple embers.

As we stepped into the main room, I nudged Alesha and pointed to the ceiling. A tangle of heavy rope nets hung across the ceiling. They looked like giant cobwebs.

Wolf stood in the centre of the long, narrow room, staring at us. He rubbed his chins again.

"Is your father at home?" Grandpa John asked impatiently. "It is urgent. Can we see him now?"

Another strange smile played over the

man's face. "You *are* seeing him!" he declared.

"I — I don't understand," Grandpa John stammered.

Wolf raised his chubby hands to his head — and tugged off the long red hair.

A wig!

Beneath the red-haired wig, he had scraggly white hair on a pink scalp.

He lowered a hand to the bottom of his face — and with a loud ripping sound, pulled off several chins.

Fakes.

He tossed the red wig and rubber chins aside and grinned at us. A slender-faced old man. "I always wanted a son," he said, "but I never had one. So I had to create him."

He really is crazy, I realized.

Totally crazy.

How can he help Alesha and me?

"It gets lonely back here in the woods," Dr Thorne said, his smile fading. "Having Wolf around makes it easier."

Grandpa John stared at the red wig spread over the floor. Then he raised his eyes to Dr Thorne. "Can you help my grandchildren?" he asked. "Do you know a cure for Full Moon Fever?"

Dr Thorne gazed at us thoughtfully. He clicked his tongue against his teeth.

I felt a wave of anger rise up through my

body. I suddenly felt like roaring at the top of my lungs. Tearing the room apart. Smashing the windows. Pulling down the nets from the ceiling and gnawing them to pieces.

I'm a monster, I told myself, struggling to fight the powerful urge to go wild.

And I'm going to stay a monster because this old man is crazy and doesn't have a clue about how to help us.

I gazed at Alesha. She was breathing hard. Her fists clenched and unclenched tensely at her sides.

She must be thinking the same things I am, I realized sadly.

Dr Thorne crossed the room to his wall of bookshelves. Humming to himself, he pulled three or four dusty old books from the shelves. Groaning under their weight, he carried them to his desk.

He plopped into his desk chair. Leaned over the desk. And began searching through the books, turning pages rapidly, running his fingers down the columns of small type.

Alesha, Grandpa John and I stood tensely in the centre of the room, watching the old man turn pages. No one said a word.

Finally, Dr Thorne raised his head. "Such tiny type is hard to read," he murmured. "I should have let Wolf read through these books. His eyes are better than mine."

98

"Did you find anything?" I demanded eagerly. "Did you find a cure?"

Dr Thorne shook his head. "No. I didn't find a cure. In fact, I didn't find Full Moon Fever. Not anywhere in these books."

Alesha and I both sighed. Grandpa John's shoulders slumped. He shut his eyes.

Dr Thorne jumped to his feet. "But I *am* going to help you," he declared.

"Help us?" I cried. "How?"

He didn't reply. Instead, he tugged a rope on the wall behind the desk.

I heard a *WHOOSH* above me.

I looked up in time to see the nets come crashing down from the ceiling.

They fell over us, so heavy they knocked the three of us to the floor.

I uttered a startled cry.

Struggled to climb up.

But the ropes were too heavy. My thrashing arms became tangled in the net. I fell back down.

Dr Thorne stood behind the desk, watching us struggle.

"Why did you trap us here?" I shouted furiously. "What are you going to do to us?"

"I'm going to make you famous."

That was Dr Thorne's reply.

I'll never forget those words. The excitement in his tiny eyes. The cruel, cold smile that spread across his pink face.

"I'm going to make you famous."

That was three weeks ago.

At least, I *think* it was three weeks. It's so hard to keep track of time when you are always travelling.

And when you live like an animal in a cage.

Yes. Alesha and I live in a cage. I think we're the lucky ones. Dr Thorne keeps Grandpa John handcuffed in a small caravan.

"I'm going to make you famous."

That's what he said.

And now we are part of a travelling carnival. People buy their tickets and stare at us as if we were zoo animals.

DR THORNE'S MONSTER KIDS.

That's what the big sign says.

THEY ONCE WERE HUMAN. NOW THEY ARE BEASTS.

People pay five dollars a ticket to see us. We're famous. We draw big crowds wherever the carnival stops.

Alesha and I are freaks. Carnival freaks.

When Dr Thorne put together the carnival, he signed up a couple of other acts. He signed a two-headed boy and a woman with a fish tail who claimed she was born in the ocean.

But they are both fakes. Their costumes aren't even very good.

Audiences aren't interested in them.

People want to see Alesha and me — the *real* monsters.

They laugh and point at us. They throw peanuts and popcorn into our cage. They shout insults and try to make us angry so that we'll roar and pound the bars and act like monsters.

They used to try to touch us, to pull our fur.

During one show, a man reached into the cage and tickled my furry feet.

I grabbed his arm and nearly pulled it off.

Now the customers have to stand behind a rope a few metres from our cage.

Alesha and I can't control our tempers. We really are animals.

We roar at the people. Sometimes we throw

101

ourselves against the bars and try to grab them.

We do everything we can to frighten them away.

But the audiences only laugh. They aren't afraid. They think it's funny.

Their laughter makes Alesha and me even more furious. But the more we growl and roar and heave our animal bodies around, the more the crowds love it.

At night, I dream about grinning faces. I hear their laughter in my dreams. I see the crowds staring at me, even in my sleep.

Now it is nearly midnight. The carnival is closed.

It is a clear, cold night. Through the cage bars, I can see the moon, nearly full, floating high in the sky.

Alesha and I are sitting on the cage floor with our backs against the bars. We are waiting for our dinner.

The cage door swings open a little way.

We turn and see Dr Thorne. He slides a big tray into the cage. The tray is piled high with raw meat.

"Enjoy your dinner," he mutters. Then he slams the cage door shut.

Every night is the same.

Every night he brings the tray of raw meat an hour after the carnival closes.

Every night he says, "Have a good dinner." Then he locks the cage door tight again.

Every night Alesha and I dive into the food. Growling and grunting, we hold the meat in our hands and rip off big chunks. We stuff the raw chunks into our mouths and swallow them whole.

We are so hungry.

So sad and hungry.

The food fills our bellies, but it doesn't make us feel any better.

We don't want to be monsters.

We want to be *us* again.

And tonight, as the cold red meat slides down my tongue, I think, *Maybe this is the last time.*

Maybe this is the last time Alesha and I will have to sit in this cage and eat like animals.

Because I have a plan.

I waited until the next night to tell my plan to Alesha.

"What a horrrrrible day." She groaned, sliding down wearily to the cage floor.

We watched the last customers file out of the carnival grounds. The bright lights dimmed. I gazed at the moon, pale and round above our cage.

"They threw banana skins." Alesha sighed. "As if we were monkeys. Those kids threw banana skins into the cage and laughed their heads off."

I slid close beside her, my eyes on Dr Thorne's trailer, which stood at the edge of the carnival grounds.

"Alesha, lisssssten," I whispered. "No more banana skins. No more of this cage."

Her eyes widened in surprise. "Robbie, what do you mean?"

"I have a plan," I whispered.

I pointed to the sky. "Look."

Alesha raised her eyes. "Look at what?"

"The moon," I replied, still pointing. "It's full. It's a full moon, Alesha. The first one since we caught Full Moon Fever."

She narrowed her eyes at me. "So?"

"Don't you remember what the old woman told Grandpa John? The cure for Full Moon Fever? We have to stand under the light of the *next* full moon. If we gaze up at the full moon, we'll be cured."

Alesha's eyes flashed excitedly. "Yessss!" she hissed. "But we have to get out of this cage. We have to stand under the moon. How?"

"Dr Thorne will be here soon with our dinner," I whispered. "He comes every night an hour after the carnival closes."

"Yes, yes, I know," Alesha growled impatiently.

"Tonight, we'll pretend to be sick. We'll lie on the cage floor and not move. He'll wonder what's wrong with us. He'll open the cage door wider. Maybe he'll even climb inside the cage to see what the problem is. Then —"

"Then we grab him, knock him out, and escape!" Alesha interrupted. "It will be so easy. Why didn't we try it before?"

"We should have," I replied. "But tonight we have no choice. Tonight we *have* to escape. In time to stand under the full moon and be cured."

"Then we'll pull Grandpa John from the caravan and get away from here for ever," Alesha added, smiling for the first time in weeks.

I glanced again at Dr Thorne's caravan. "Get ready," I instructed Alesha. "It's almost time for him to bring us our dinner."

We stretched out on the cage floor. Alesha sprawled on her back. I stayed on my side so that I could watch for Dr Thorne.

We didn't move.

We waited.

And waited.

The full moon rose higher in the purple night sky. I could hear the whisper of the wind through the bare trees. Carnival tents flapped in the breeze.

We waited.

I watched the dark caravan. I could see a light in the window. Dr Thorne was in there.

Why wasn't he coming out? Why wasn't he bringing us our nightly meal?

And then I realized.

I sat up. "Alesha — he isn't coming tonight," I murmured.

She let out a gasp. She remained on her back on the cage floor. "What do you mean? He *has* to come!" she cried.

"He knows," I told her through gritted teeth. "He knows tonight is the full moon. He knows tonight is the only night we can be cured — and he doesn't want us cured!"

I groaned. "Don't you see? He wants to keep us as monsters. For ever. So he won't be coming with our dinner. He won't be opening the cage door tonight."

Alesha sat up.

I caught the fear in her eyes.

"Robbie," she whispered, gazing at the sky. "Look. The moon is almost at its peak. We have so little time. What are we going to do?"

I gazed through the bars at Dr Thorne's caravan.

A monster for ever, I thought.

I raised my eyes to the moon.

I thought about the laughing, jeering audiences. The stares. The stupid jokes they shouted at Alesha and me.

The banana skins.

A monster for ever.

I stared again at Dr Thorne's caravan.

He isn't coming tonight, I thought.

He isn't coming.

I felt something inside me snap.

My chest heaved up and down. A wave of anger made my whole body shudder.

I had to shout. I had to roar. Or else my head would explode.

I tilted my face to the sky, opened my mouth, and let my fury out in a deafening howl.

I turned and saw Alesha standing beside me, howling too, shouting out her anger.

And then, without saying a word to each other, we threw ourselves against the cage door.

Snarling like enraged animals, we tore at the bars. Chewed them with our jagged teeth. Ripped at them with our big, fur-covered hands. Kicked and thrashed.

Our anger gave us strength we never had before.

The metal bars bent in our hands. The lock snapped. The door swung open.

With excited cries, we dived out, side by side. On to the paved path beside the cage.

Under the moonlight.

I grabbed Alesha's hand. We moved to the grass. The soft grass . . . away from the cage . . . away from our prison.

"Look up at the moon," I ordered. "We're just in time. Just in time to be cured."

But I heard a shout.

I spun round — and saw Dr Thorne running from his caravan. He frantically waved one hand in front of him.

What was that in his hand?

A whip?

Yes. Did he plan to whip us like wild animals? Whip us back into the cage?

"Back!" he shouted breathlessly. "Get back!"

His big stomach bounced in front of him as he ran.

He crossed the path. Came at us over the grass.

Raised the whip high.

Alesha and I both pounced on him.

He uttered a startled gasp as the whip flew from his hand.

He never had a chance to swing it.

We leaped on him. Knocked him on his back.

And then with our new strength, the wild strength of our anger, we picked him up, lifted his huge body as if it were weightless.

We carried him — struggling, kicking, shouting at us — to an empty cage. We heaved him inside. I slammed the cage door shut. Alesha snapped the lock.

"Hurry!" I choked out, turning to Alesha.

I gazed up at the full moon.

"Hurry — not much time left."

Alesha and I ran back to the grass. Standing side by side, we turned our heads to the moonlight.

We let it pour over us, so soft and silvery.

Would it work?

Would it cure us?

No.

We stood under the moonlight for what seemed like hours.

The wind rustled our fur. The canvas carnival tents flapped behind us.

No. No. No...

It didn't work. The cold silvery light washed over our animal bodies. But we didn't change back to Robbie and Alesha.

We didn't change at all.

With a howl of disappointment, I spun back to our cage. Dr Thorne was shaking the door, trying to pull it open.

"Come back, you two!" he called. "You have nowhere else to go. This is your home now!"

"Noooooooooo!" Another howl of horror escaped my throat.

No — never. This cannot be our home.

Alesha and I raced across the grass. We burst breathlessly into the caravan where Grandpa John was held prisoner.

He jumped to his feet. "You escaped!" he cried happily. "But —"

We didn't let him finish his sentence. With my new strength, I ripped the handcuffs from his wrists. "Let's go!" I growled.

"Where?" Grandpa John asked, following us out of the caravan.

"Home," I replied.

Alesha and I flew in the cargo hold again.

We hardly spoke during the entire flight home. We were too unhappy, too worried about what our future would be like.

Our future as monsters. . .

Grandpa John rented a van when we landed. Alesha sat up front beside him. She slumped low in the seat so no one would see her. I hunched behind them, picking at the fur on the back of my hand.

"I wired your parents before we took off," Grandpa John announced, guiding the van on to the highway. "I told them you were both in good health. But I warned them they were in for a horrible shock."

A horrible shock?

What will Mum and Dad do when they see us like this? I wondered.

And how will they feel when we lose control one day and rip the whole house to pieces?

Or when we eat the dog?

Scruffy. . .

Scruffy flashed into my mind. That cute little guy.

I can't wait to see Scruffy, I thought.

My stomach growled.

I uttered a gasp. I hope I don't eat Scruffy, I thought.

Will I be able to control my monster hunger around him?

I'm so hungry right now, I thought. I'm so hungry *all* the time.

We pulled into our driveway. Alesha pushed open her door and slid out. But I didn't want to leave the car.

I didn't want Mum and Dad to see me covered in fur, with jagged teeth poking out of my long animal snout.

"Come on, Robbie," Grandpa John urged softly. He held the door open for me. "I'll help you explain to your parents."

To my surprise, Mum and Dad weren't at home.

"I didn't tell them when we were arriving," Grandpa John said. "They'll probably be back soon."

I heard a yip, then wild barking.

Scruffy came tearing into the room. His tail

wagging frantically, he jumped to greet Alesha, then came leaping at me.

"Scruffy!" I cried. I lifted him into my arms. He licked my furry face.

"He doesn't care that we're monsters!" Alesha exclaimed. "He recognizes us. He doesn't care that we're all furry!"

"I hope Mum and Dad are like Scruffy," I declared. I hugged the dog tightly.

And felt my stomach gnawing. Suddenly felt so hungry. . .

Starving. . .

Scruffy licked my snout. I held him up in front of me.

I started to drool.

Starving. . .

Whoa! Wait! I don't WANT to eat Scruffy!

The trick-or-treat sweets flashed into my mind.

Was my Halloween bag still in my room?

My stomach growled again.

I set Scruffy down and went tearing up the stairs to my room.

Yes!

The bag was on the chair where I had left it.

I grabbed it with both hands. Tore the bag apart.

Sweets fell all over the floor. I began hungrily shoving them into my open jaws. I didn't stop to remove the wrappers.

I gobbled them up. Handful after handful.

And then I lowered my gaze to the floor. "Scruffy — stop!" I cried, swallowing a big gob of chocolate.

The dog had a bar between his teeth. He was gnawing frantically on the wrapper.

"No! Not good for dogs!" I growled. "Remember last year?"

I swiped it away from him. "Hey!" The red-and-yellow wrapper caught my eye.

I stopped chewing.

I raised the bar close to my face and gaped at it.

I read the name on the wrapper again.

And then read it again.

"Alesha!" I screamed. "Alesha — come here — *hurry*! I — I don't *believe* this!"

27

Alesha came racing into my room. Scruffy ran up to her, his little tail swinging excitedly.

"Robbie — what's wrong?" Alesha cried.

"This chocolate bar —" I stammered, holding it up. "The bar Mrs Eakins gave us on Halloween!"

"The Best bar?" Alesha asked, her eyes on the red-and-yellow wrapper in my trembling hand. "What about it?"

Scruffy shoved his nose into the trick-or-treat bag. I picked him up and pushed him aside.

"It isn't a Best bar!" I told Alesha breathlessly.

"Excuse me?"

"I read it wrong," I explained. "It was dark and very late, remember? And I read the name wrong, Alesha. Check it out."

I threw the chocolate bar to her.

"It's not a Best bar," I cried. "It's a BEAST bar!"

Alesha studied the wrapper. She read the name softly. "Beast bar."

The bar fell from her hand. Her mouth dropped open in shock. "You mean —?"

"I mean we don't have Full Moon Fever," I replied. "The old woman in the woods told the truth. There's no such thing as Full Moon Fever."

"The Beast bar —" Alesha murmured.

"Mrs Eakins hated us," I continued. "So she gave us these bars — and turned us into *beasts*!"

Alesha thought about it for a long time. Her eyes darted excitedly from side to side as she thought.

And then she tilted her head back and let out a furious roar.

Before I realized it, I was roaring too.

We both stood there in the middle of my room, roaring out our anger.

And then, without saying a word to each other, we turned and ran. Ran down the stairs. Past Grandpa John, who uttered a startled gasp as we flew through the living room. Out of the front door.

Still roaring out our fury, we ran down the block. We crossed the street without stopping. And kept running.

"What arrrrre we doing?" I finally called to Alesha. Even though I already knew the answer.

"We're going to show Mrs Eakins what a beast can do!"

We stormed across her front lawn. Leaped on to the front doorstep.

We didn't knock or ring the bell.

With a furious snarl, I grabbed the front door — and ripped it off its hinges.

Then we plunged into the living room, growling, grunting, panting hard. Ready for action.

"Mrs Eeeeeakins!" I roared.

No reply.

I dived to the wall, ripped a painting off its hook, shoved my furry fist through it, and heaved it to the floor.

Alesha lurched to the sofa. She ripped the green fabric apart with her teeth.

Then, laughing like a hyena, she began pulling out the stuffing with both hands.

I ripped apart another painting. Then I shoved my fist through the wall. I started tearing off strips of wallpaper.

Gooooood. It felt so good.

It felt so right!

"Mrs Eeeeeeeakins!" I roared again.

Alesha pulled a clump of flowers from a tall vase and shoved them into her mouth. She smashed the vase against the wall.

"Did somebody call me?"

A voice from the back hallway.

Alesha spat out the flowers she was eating. I spun away from the wall I had destroyed.

Mrs Eakins, dressed in black, strolled casually into the room.

She didn't seem to care about the damage we had done. A pleased smile spread over her pale face.

"Well, well. My two little beasts," she said coldly. "I hope you had a good Halloween."

We didn't reply.

With a furious snarl, Alesha leaped at the woman. She wrapped her furry hands round Mrs Eakins's throat.

Mrs Eakins uttered a choked gasp and staggered back against the wall.

Alesha roared and tightened her grip.

I roared too.

We were animals now. We were total beasts, no longer human.

I took off, running across the room to help Alesha finish off the struggling, choking woman.

120

"Oww!" I cried out as I knocked over a small cabinet.

The cabinet drawers came crashing out.

And I stared down at — *chocolate bars*!

The drawers were filled with bars in blue-and-white wrappers.

"Hunnnh?" I bent and picked one up.

And my eyes froze on the label: CURE BAR.

Yesssss!

The cabinet was filled with Cure bars! Bars that would cure Alesha and me!

I grabbed up a handful of them. Then I turned to Alesha.

"Stop!" I ordered her. "Alesha — let Mrs Eakins go!"

Alesha spun round in surprise. "What?"

Her hands slid off the woman's throat.

"I've got the cure!" I called to my sister. "We can go! Come on! We'll be cured! We'll be normal again!"

I waved the Cure bars over my head. And uttered a gleeful, happy shout. Then I stuffed one into my mouth and gobbled it down.

Alesha came running across the room. She grabbed up a handful of bars. She ate one of them, chewing noisily.

Then we both started to the front door.

I turned to Mrs Eakins. "I hope you've learned your lesson!" I snarled. "I hope you've learned never to use your powers on kids again!"

121

Mrs Eakins rubbed her throat. She stared at us angrily.

Then she waved a hand at us, waved it as if casting a spell. "Smaller and smaller," she called out hoarsely, still rubbing her throat. "You will both grow smaller and smaller."

"Afraid that won't work!" I cried happily. "My sister and I have both eaten Cure bars — and we have enough of them to last us a long, long time!"

Alesha and I ran through the open doorway. Down the front lawn. Leaping. Jumping for joy.

So happy. So happy.

We had nearly made it to the street when I began to feel funny. Strange. Tingly all over.

I tripped over my jeans.

My feet came out of my huge shoes.

Huge shoes? Why were my clothes suddenly too big?

I turned to Alesha. I could see her shrinking!

Her face filled with horror. "We — we're getting smaller!" she stammered. Her voice was suddenly tiny and high.

"But — but —" I sputtered.

"Let's eat another Cure bar — fast!" Alesha cried. She raised a bar to her face.

And then her mouth dropped open and her eyes bulged wide.

"Robbie —" she gasped. "Robbie — you've done it again!"

"Huh?" I stared at her. And then I lowered my eyes and read the name on the wrapper:

Curse bar.